I0724243

The Master of Harmlessness...
who came and told us something
about our real selves.

Ingo Swann (1933-2013) was an American artist and exceptionally successful subject in parapsychology experiments. As a child he spontaneously had numerous paranormal experiences, mostly of the OBE type, the future study of which became a major passion as he matured. In 1970, he began acting as a parapsychology test subject in tightly controlled laboratory settings with numerous scientific researchers. Because of the success of most of these thousands of test trials, major media worldwide often referred, to him as "the scientific psychic." His subsequent research on behalf of American intelligence interests, including that of the CIA, won him top PSI-spy status. His involvement in government research projects required the discovery of innovative approaches toward the actual realizing of subtle human energies. He viewed PSI powers as only parts of the larger spectrum of human sensing systems and was internationally known as an advocate and researcher of the exceptional powers of the human mind.

To learn more about Ingo, his work, art, and other books, please visit: **www.ingoswann.com**.

MASTER OF HARMLESSNESS

A BIOMIND SUPERPOWERS BOOK
PUBLISHED BY

Swann-Ryder Productions, LLC
www.ingoswann.com

Copyright © 2021 by Swann-Ryder Productions, LLC.

All rights reserved. No part of this book may be used or reproduced in any manner whatsoever without written permission. For more information address: www.ingoswann.com.

First edition BioMind Superpowers Books.

ISBN-13: 978-1-949214-04-8

Cover art: *Kismet 3*
by Ingo Swann © Swann-Ryder Productions, LLC.

Interior art: Shutterstock.com

Lotus Flower © Tierre3012 | *Landscape* © Susii | *Palace County* © Susii | *Mediating Buddha* © Elina Li | *Chinese Butterfly* © Susii | *Abstract Mountain* © marukopum | *Circle* © sunwart | *All Seeing Eye* © SHIK_SHIK | *Set of Black Dots* © Kirichenko Diana | *Angel Wings* © Sayasouk | *Light Rays* © Valeriya_Dor | *Abstract Swirl* © Sayasouk

Names, characters, businesses, places, events, locales, and incidents are either the products of Ingo Swann's imagination or used in a fictitious manner. Any resemblance to actual persons, living or dead, or actual events is purely coincidental.

MASTER OF HARMLESSNESS

INGO SWANN

PUBLISHER'S NOTE

Master of Harmlessness is a work of fiction, the pages of which were found shortly after Ingo died in 2013, bound together with a rubber band. However, for reasons that cannot be explained, then, or now, the manuscript was not sent to the University of West Georgia to be included in his archives. It had a purpose; we just did not know what.

But then a chance thing occurred late in 2020. In listening to a segment of Ingo's 1995 interview on *21st Century Radio* with Dr. Bob Hieronimus, we learned that this short story, or tale as Ingo would call it, was a sort of accompaniment to his *Purple Fables*. Whereas *Purple Fables* would be published soon after Ingo completed it, this work was not.

It was this voice of Ingo's, from a moment in time in the not-so-distant past, that served as a reminder of a thing yet still needing attending to, and most assuredly with great haste.

With Ingo's words still lingering in our minds as much as in our hearts, we are tremendously honored to publish this book in his memory. More so though, we are exceedingly grateful to *21st Century Radio*, Dr. Bob Hieronimus, and Laura Cortner for unearthing this marvelous golden key, and continuing to share Ingo's words and ideas with the world.

AUTHOR'S NOTE

In April, I woke up one morning, out of the blue, and there was a sort of voice in my head, not exactly a voice, but sort of a telepathic thing, saying, "You will now write the *Purple Fables*, there will be four of them, and you will do one in each day and the title is to be *Purple Fables*," and I said okay...they were sort of dictated from somebody else, someplace, I guess.

The *Purple Fables* happened in April of 1993, but on Christmas morning I woke up and there were these guys again, or these whatever, saying "Okay now you are going to write a thing called the *Tale of the Master of Harmlessness* and it's to be seventy-six draft pages in length," which is actually the length of all four *Purple Fables* put together, "and you are to work on it for certain hours in the day, and it will all be done by New Year's."

And in fact it was done and printed out and sit there in manuscript form on December 31st.

-- **Ingo Swann**
Interview with Dr. Bob Hieronimus
21st Century Radio
February 5, 1995

For my niece.
Remember...love is
the most important thing.

CONTENTS

Translation Note — i

The Statement Fragment — xi

The Tale of the Master of Harmlessness

THE ARRIVAL OF THE MASTER — 1

THE BEGINNING OF THE GATHERING — 7

TRYING TO FIND OUT ABOUT THE MASTER — 10

THE BEGINNING OF THE ILLUMINATION — 16

THE MASTER SPEAKS ABOUT "THE WAY" — 21

THE MASTER'S "LIFE-UNIT" MESSAGE — 24

THE MASTER SPEAKS ABOUT THE MIRACULOUS — 28

THE EXTRUDING OF THE DEMONS AND THE CLEANSING — 32

THE APPEARANCE OF THE ANGELS — 39

THE COMMUNION AND THE RAPTURE — 45

THE DEPARTURE OF THE MASTER — 48

TRANSLATION NOTE

During the early part of the twentieth century, a very old manuscript was found in what was then called Mongolia. Mongolia became known simply as Area 15 of the Greater Asian Republic after the world reorganization that took place early in our twenty-first century. Mongolia had always been largely decertified and thinly populated, but today Asian Area 15 is completely uninhabitable due to the savage world-wide ecological shifts that took place between 2006 and 2010.

The manuscript contains the narrated tale of a "Master" and describes a series of unique and inexplicable events attributed to him. There is no clue to the narrator's identity in the text. The narrator apparently witnessed the remarkable phenomena, and later made a complete record of the happenings. There is also nothing in the narrative that would permit us to determine when or where the events happened.

The age of the manuscript is entirely questionable. Why this is so needs to be presented because it is meaningful as to the age of the narration. The circumstances of the manuscript's discovery are not well documented. But it appears first to have been found in about 1910, beneath floorboards of an ancient Buddhist monastery outside of Urga (later called Ulaanbaatar), the former capital city of Mongolia.

The manuscript's discovery aroused great interest at first. But the manuscript remained incompletely translated after some scholars indicated that it was a clever fake, but without explaining why or how such a "fake" could have been manufactured.

In any event, what then happened to the manuscript is not clear.

After the death of the Eighth Jebtsundamba Living Buddha in 1924, and with no discovered successor to take his place, Mongolia was cast into destructive political turmoil.

First the Mongolian People's Revolutionary Party took hold, followed by Mongolia's occupation by the Japanese between 1931 and 1945. Next, the country was largely destroyed by the Chinese civil war in the years leading to 1950, and then decimated by the Communist takeover.

It was throughout these upheavals that most religious centers and precious artifacts were deliberately destroyed.

The manuscript, having thought to have been destroyed or lost, somehow escaped the Communist destruction of religious artifacts, and was next found in India during the millennial year 2000, just before the great climactic catastrophe. How it came to be in India was not recorded.

At that point, several photocopies were made at the request of interested scholars, and these were sent abroad for study and translation. Only two of those photocopies can be found today, some forty years later, while the fate of the manuscript itself is uncertain. It may have been lost during the internal wars that convulsed the sub-continent in the first and second decades of the present century.

The manuscript was of a single length of vegetable parchment. The process of manufacturing was not determined. But the manuscript showed no signs of having deteriorated either in 1910 or in 2000, and so the process of manufacturing must have included some remarkable preserving techniques.

This single length had remained supple and measured nineteen inches high by six feet long and was folded accordion style into widths of five inches to make the "pages."

The folds remained flexible, and so the whole could be opened up and refolded with ease.

The inks or paints were of red pigments and the folded whole was bound between slightly larger wood slats covered with beaten gold, and embellished with jewels, three of which were large diamonds, but which otherwise incorporated no design elements. The writing on the parchment was exceedingly small as to require a magnifying glass. As existing photographs show, the whole of this "book," though long and narrow, was small and compact and could be balanced in one hand.

As its first page, it contained an explanation (which is herein referred to as the "Statement Fragment") which indicated the circumstances as to how the manuscript had come about. But this first page had undergone some destruction, which may have been deliberate. The rest of the manuscript was completely intact.

The *Statement Fragment* tells that the manuscript was made at the command of the Ancient One, but does not identify when, and so this does not help in dating the manuscript.

The *Statement Fragment* indicates that the manuscript is a translation from another ancient language of a far older manuscript which was in the process of decomposing. Except that it was being eaten by worms, the far older manuscript is not described regarding its materials or composition, and the more ancient language is not specified or named.

According to the *Statement Fragment*, the older decomposing text was first copied in its original language. After this, a second translated text was made, and which is the one found in 1910, and later photocopied in 2000. The language of this second text is

Uralic, or proto-Uralic, showing many Altaic connectives, while Ural-Altaic was the essential language of central Asia east of the Ural mountains, including Tibet.

The wooden slats themselves were of a particular acacia tree found only in higher plains of the middle Africa veldt, but the Uralic language of the translation is indigenous to the High Asian Mountains. Uncertainty regarding the original manuscript's origin abound as in particular:

- ೞ The wood of the slats was African in origin.
- ೞ This may indicate that the older original text had not been produced in Asia, but may have been imported into Asia, and at some point, obviously into Mongolia where it was translated into proto-Uralic.
- ೞ At that point, it may be that the wooden slats belonging to the original decomposing version were reused after it was copied to bind the new Uralic translation, in which case the original old text was as small and compact as the newer translation.
- ೞ From indications in the *Statement Fragment*, it may be that the *copy made in the original language* was not put into perishable materials, but incised onto gold tablets[1] for imperishable storage.
- ೞ If this was the case, then the new gold plates would not necessarily need the original wooden-gold-pounded covers—and which then might have been used to help protect the translation into proto-Uralic.

---

[1] The existence of such "gold tablets" has never been discovered, and no mention of them is discernable in any other available source.

Carbon dating of the parchment pages appears not to have been undertaken, since too much would have been destroyed in the process. But carbon dating of a small segment of the slats (conducted in 2001) indicates a time-window of approximately 900 B.C.E. plus or minus 100 years. The slats at least are pre-Buddhic (Buddha lived probably from 563 to 483 B.C.E.).

However, this does not establish the age of either the original text or the translated copy. There are other complications in ascertaining this age regarding both the lost original text and the later (but still very old) proto-Uralic version of which only two photocopies remain today.

The chief objections made in 1910, regarding the manuscript's authenticity, were that it mentions the use of some electronic equipment which did not exist until after 1877.

The proto-Uralic version indicates the use by the Master of what appears to be something like a microphone, and a public address system, and specifically indicates the whining noise typical of some kind of amplifier or loudspeaker. Microphones were not invented until circa 1877.

Literally translated, the relevant words indicate a "voice enlarger making loud speaking over the countryside" and which herein has been translated as "microphone" and "public address system."

Likewise, the text refers to something that seems like the telephones in very wide use during the twentieth century, but which have since been replaced by our hologram units (HoloU). Literally translated, the relevant words in this case are "the going and coming voices over the land."

"Voices" are specified, but images are not, and so the best serviceable concept is the telephone or at least some other similar telephonic equipment.

Since nothing of either kind of electronic equipment existed throughout known human history until 1877, we are thus left with either of three options:

1. The use in translation of microphone, etc., may not be correct;
2. If correct, the manuscript may be a contrived fake (as some said in 1910), and which caused the early disinterest in the document; or
3. The original lost-language version was written in some far more remote prehistorical period in which advanced technologies (i.e., electronic broadcasting and communications techniques) were in hand—but the technical knowledge of which was later lost.

The latter option has led some to speculate that the original lost text was of enormously greater antiquity, perhaps pre-Flood, and had originated in Atlantis, which many believe to have possessed electronic knowledge, and that the language of the original text was "Atlantean." But no Atlantean language has ever been verified as having existed, even in rudimentary form.

The manuscript has several linguistic problems, none of which were resolved until this present translation. But these linguistic problems need to be presented ultimately to help in understanding.

The Master's title has caused translation problems. In the proto-Uralic version he is literally referred to as "the Master who makes the quality of little harming (or hurting)." It was assumed (in 1910 and again in 2001) that this should be translated as a "master of peace."

But this assumption resulted in contextual problems in translating other parts of the text into contemporary language formats. For upon inspection the proto-Uralic term for "peace" is found nowhere in the text (although the term for "war" is found).

Since the *quality* of "making little harming" should be rendered as *harmlessness* (-ness indicating a quality), the title for the Master is herein given as the Master of Harmlessness. This usage reduces many contextual problems that would otherwise continue to exist.

Another translation problem is as follows. Very few, if any, languages from antiquity contain words referring to the *subjective* realms of mind or consciousness as such. In the greater past, no special distinctions were made between the objective and subjective realms.

Clinical distinctions between objective (real) and subjective (imaginary) only began to be made during the so-called "modern" nineteenth and twentieth centuries (but which since 2025 have been referred to as the Dark Age of Modern Science).

The clinical "modern" distinction unfortunately resulted in the overvaluing of objective (real-concrete) experience and the undervaluing of subjective (unreal-imaginary) experience, even to the degree of completely alienating the subjective's true and vital importance in reality-making and reality-perceiving.

In antiquity, the subjective experience was literally as real as was the objective experience, and so no special words evolved to distinguish between the two.

Early efforts to translate the manuscript found in 1910 floundered because of anachronistic attempts to utilize the modern words *mind* and *consciousness*. This then required the "understanding" that the extraordinary phenomena produced by the Master (and witnessed as objectively real and concrete by those present) were unreal and only imaginary. This was not workable, because in fact the concepts of *mind* and *consciousness* do not exist in the manuscript, and so they are not needed in translation.

This difficulty has fortunately been overcome in the present translation.

The term in the Uralic text that caused the mind-consciousness difficulty is a combined word which apparently meant, when literally translated, something like "thought-substance" meaning that thought has substance, and that this substance is real and objective.

Although this combined term is a little unwieldy in English, it has been utilized in order to conform to the obvious intent of the tale. Otherwise, and to help reduce anachronistic tendencies, passé modern terms, such as mind and consciousness, are therefore avoided in this translation.

The use, however, of the term "rapture" remains questionable regarding the intent of the narrative. No exact meaning in translation has ever been identified regarding the proto-Uralic term used in the text.

But it is apparently derived from two root words meaning (1) "lifting" or "outgoing upward," and (2) "ecstasy" or "thought-substance-harmony." Here we have to bear in mind that it's not unusual to have to employ a string of English words to approximate a single world that was familiarly used in antiquity.

Literally expressed then the Uralic term means thought-substance, ecstasy-lifting, outgoing upward, harmony.

The English term *rapture* is the best approximate single word that might mean this.

Rapture typically means an expression or manifestation of ecstasy or passion. During the Middle Ages, however, when capitalized, it came to refer (1) to salvation of the good at the End of the Times, and (2) the lifting or transporting of the good into a Utopia of peace and tranquility and harmony and prosperity.

This Utopia was literally taken as another world or realm in some kind of "Above," and was often referred to as Heaven or heavenlike. In the Uralic text, thought-substance-harmony might be seen as utopian-esque in nature, and so the general term *rapture* is utilized.

All of these linguistic matters have caused disputes among scholars and translators.

However, when fully translated, the narrative obviously describes a "transcendence event" of some kind, and which was both subjectively and objectively experienced by those present at the time.

Thus, the entire tale of the Master of Harmlessness is a *rapture* story and is herein presented as such.

What might be taken as representing chapter headings exist in the proto-Uralic text, but chapter numbers do not, and these have been introduced for convenience.

— The Department of Proto-Consciousness Studies
Central World University
March 2048

THE STATEMENT FRAGMENT

<u>THE MOST HOLY LIVING ANCIENT ONE</u> has commanded the preservation of the record from the most ancient times of the Master of Harmlessness which has been eaten by too many worms.

<u>THE MOST HOLY LIVING ANCIENT ONE</u> has again commanded that the record from the most ancient times of the Master of Harmlessness also be cast into Our Great Tongue [so as] to be spoken once each year when the winter-cold Sun prepares to dress in new life [i.e. the spring equinox].

<u>THE MOST HOLY LIVING ANCIENT ONE</u> commands that all tribes gather together and listen, and that emissaries go to the outward regions and speak the most ancient memory-record to all.

<u>THE MOST HOLY LIVING ANCIENT ONE</u> commands that [part destroyed] . . . so that the times before the Great Ice Mountains and Oceans should not be [part destroyed].

<u>THE MOST HOLY</u> [part destroyed] . . . commands that the great Second and Third Books of the most ancient times likewise [part destroyed] . . . preserved by carving into gold tablets and placed [part destroyed] . . . until after the Great Cataclysms . . . [remainder of the page destroyed.]

The Tale of the Master of Harmlessness

"First, do as little harm as possible."
(Attributed to the Master of Harmlessness)

"There are no secrets.
There is no mystery.
There is only common sense."
(An ancient Onondaga proverb)

"Seeking bits of identity in history's vast abyss."
(Ingo Swann)

1

THE ARRÍVAL ÖF THE MASTER

There came one day to our small town, a Master, who was passing through, and walking from some forgotten place to another unknown one.

He wasn't at first recognized as a Master, of course, for such are rare and unfamiliar. But his dress was different, and not in the present style, and these clothes of his were worn and dirty. He was out of place, strange, foreign.

Now, our town is a good place. But as elsewhere, what's strange and foreign stands out as not belonging, and people like to get rid of what doesn't belong. So some young boys, having little else to amuse them, first threw rocks and pebbles at the Master because his dress was different and didn't belong, and perhaps because these children had already been taught to distrust what's different.

But the Master merely smiled and laughed in good cheer, and threw back a rock or two. These thrown-back rocks and pebbles then did stop in mid-air before hitting anyone, and fell harmlessly to the ground. This confused the boys who didn't know what to think, or do, and so they went further along in the street and found other mischief to amuse their unformed minds.

The town's sheriff, though, had noticed this rock-throwing, because it's his job to see all, and whatever goes on. And since this sheriff kept the peace and protected our town from vagrants, and other undesirables, he went up to the Master to investigate him, as he was supposed to do.

This Master then said that he was on a walking trip and was merely tired and would rest for a while in our little park, which had flowers and a fountain in it—and when rested he would again be on his walking way.

Now the sheriff didn't know if walking-trips were illegal or not; but it seemed that people could freely walk in our town and as well in our great land, which stretched from mountain to mountain and all that was in between. So there was nothing yet illegal to be seen or dealt with. The sheriff advised that the Master should be on his walking way before nightfall for it was illegal for anyone to sleep out-of-doors within our town's city limits.

Then this Master went into our small park and sat himself on a bench beside the fountain and closed his eyes as if in rest.

But it was these eyes, which began the commotion. For in passing into our small park, this Master passed three ladies out doing their shopping, and these same three ladies were principal ladies in our town, and they made it their business to watch and see everything that happened, too.

These three shopping ladies began gossiping about the Master's appearance, which at first was distasteful to them. And they frowned and worried if he had some disease that might spread about. And then they went on to imagine the dangers that unkempt strangers might bring with them.

But this Master otherwise seemed handsome and virile enough, and so these ladies, as ladies like to do, giggled, and wondered what this stranger might look like if he was cleaned and scrubbed up.

"His strange blue eyes *do* seem wild enough," said the first lady to the other two.

"Oh," said the second lady, "but his eyes are brown and fearsome, as I distinctly saw when he passed us along the street."

But the third lady laughed and chided: "No, you silly girls, his eyes *are* wild and fearsome—but they are dark green and glowing. I've never seen such green glowing eyes in all my life."

Now, shopping ladies pride themselves on their accurate senses in order not to be cheated or something else worse, and so they notice everything. And so they discussed this problem of the Master's eyes, but whom they yet thought was nothing more than an unkempt vagrant.

In the end of these discussions, there was nothing else to do to resolve the situation but to walk through the park and pass near the fountain so they could again glimpse those eyes. This they contrived so as the Master wouldn't notice the deliberateness of their looking at him. And as they passed near the fountain, the Master opened his eyes so the three ladies could briefly look into them.

"Blue, indeed," whispered the first lady.

"Nonsense," said the second. "Definitely brown!"

"But can't you see the glowing green?" asked the third.

Now, here was a *situation*, and principal ladies in small towns such as ours like to get situations straightened out and ensure that everyone knows about what takes place. So these three ladies went across the street to the sheriff who, ever on guard, had seen them in the park looking closely at the Master.

Our sheriff thought that the three principal ladies had come to complain about the Master, and so he said defensively: "He's on a walking trip, and that's not illegal, and there's nothing I can do about it."

"Oh, but we don't care about that," said the ladies. "But did you notice the color of his eyes?"

"Well, yes I did," responded the sheriff. "His eyes *are* strange enough, being dark red. I'll swear I've never seen eyes of that kind before. He must be from some foreign parts or somewhere else."

Now, nothing much unusual happens in our small town, and so the unusual, when it does come about, naturally takes the interest of everyone, even if the matter is small. So the sheriff and the three ladies stared across the street and into our small park, and tried their best to inspect the Master more closely without his realizing it.

Now this small matter of a resting Master got more complicated because of what happened next. In our small park lived some squirrels, as is not unusual, and a flock of pigeons and other kinds of birds that pecked and ate. Now it was seen that the squirrels were sitting on the Master's knees or his shoulders, and the pigeons were not pecking and eating but silently stood on the ground around the Master's feet.

"Maybe," the first lady worried, "he'll catch and eat them for his dinner." And so here was a danger potential for the sheriff to investigate, and this he went to do with the three ladies in tow.

"Seems you've got a way with creatures," said the sheriff to the Master.

In turn the Master smiled and said "Well, these are not creatures but little beings and I love them all and so they know I'll not harm them in anyway, and so wherever I go on my walking way, such as these, little beings come up and talk to me."

No one in our small town, of course, had ever heard or thought of such a thing. And so, in their surprise and incomprehension none of the four investigators knew what to say or do.

Finally, feeling himself somewhat stupid, the sheriff asked: "Then you mean no harm to these creatures?"

"Oh, most certainly not!" exclaimed the Master. "It's my first purpose, along my walking way, as it is through my life itself, never to create harm. Harmlessness is a virtue, and all should try to practice it."

At this none of the four investigators now knew what to say, and this was for sure, because none of them had ever heard of the virtue called harmlessness because no one had ever taught or even preached it.

So then followed a silence, during which more squirrels and pecking birds came along, and some small park mice, and then some butterflies, which alighted on the Master's head.

Then, since no one was saying anything, but just looking, the Master said: "All life beings are very wonderful, you know. These small ones here are wonderful, but all beings are wonderful, too. You four here are wonderful, as is everyone, even though they probably don't realize it—as even I, at one time, did not."

By now other citizens of our small town had noticed something unusual going on in the park, and they began coming up to see and watch what it was. The first principal lady whispered to the newcomers that "he says we're all wonderful even though we might not know it," and the newcomers in turn whispered this to others coming up to watch and see.

The second principal lady whispered that he was a man of harmlessness, and that this, whatever it was, was a virtue, even though in our wonderfulness we hadn't ever heard of it.

The principal third lady, not to be outdone in this whispering, said his eyes were seen of a different color by any who looked at them.

2

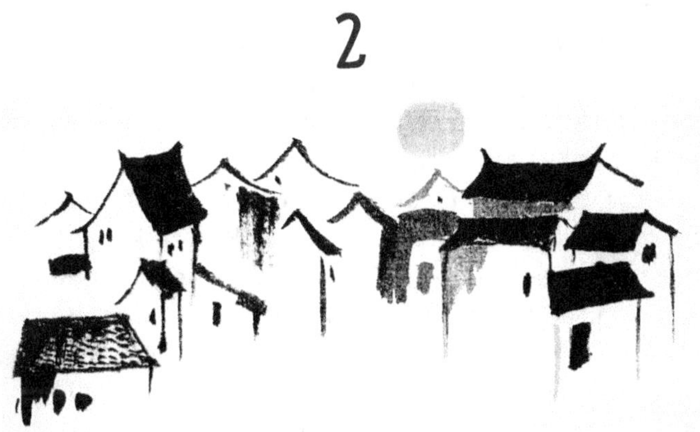

THE BEGINNING OF THE GATHERING

And so more and more newcomers tried to get closer to see the different colored eyes. But they had to take care not to step on the little beings, which themselves were watching the Master as if they were enraptured, more and more of which were arriving, too.

Now it was seen that the Master had a nice beard, soft and curling with some grey hairs hanging in it. Yet his face was young enough, and when he smiled at the small beings gathering it seemed to get younger even more.

Now each of the three ladies decided they must do something, since ladies don't feel good if they're not doing, and so the first one asked: "Are you hungry? Shall we bring you some food?"

"Oh, heaven's no," replied the Master. "I don't want to be a bother in passing through your town. I don't eat much, for the air mostly sustains me, and the squirrels will bring me some of their hidden nuts if I ask for them."

But the ladies were disappointed at this because they don't like doing nothing, and seeing this disappointment the

Master said: "But I could use some good clean water, which is hard to come upon in these polluted days." So there was now a small rush to find some clean water, and when this was found the Master duly drank some of it, but not a whole lot, and he thanked all kindly, and smiled.

Now the Master began to seem friendly and kind, and so the first lady got up her courage to ask him about the true color of his eyes, and he replied that this depended on many things, and also who was looking at them.

"People," he said, "see things in many different ways depending on how they see what they do in the first place."

This now needed to be explained a little more, and so the Master said that a lot exists that no one sees at all, or only rarely so, and that people seldom worry about what they don't see, and that this non-seeing has something to do with what they do see.

This wasn't understood very well, and so someone asked for an example of what wasn't seen.

"Well," said the Master, "love is not usually seen. It is felt, but not seen, and thus people don't see that everything around them that lives and grows does so in an atmosphere of love, and nothing else, since nothing will grow in an atmosphere of hate."

And the Master went on: "Wherever growing things are, they must also breathe and recirculate the air of love, for if this air is absent then they can't and won't grow at all. So life and love are inseparable. Yet many see the life around them but don't see the love that's absolutely necessary for it."

By now, many more people had gathered, and some of those who had first gathered, and who had seen and watched, had made some quick trips to nearby telephones to tell others what was happening. Soon telephones were talking everywhere in our town and to places outside of it, and the listeners thought they had just as well stop what they were doing and go see this interesting thing.

Meanwhile, in the park some now wanted to sit nearer to the Master so as to hear him better. Our park benches were few in number, and these, and the fountain rim, were already mostly occupied with the creatures, who also seemed to be listening.

So these little listening creatures somehow had delicately to be pushed aside for people to sit themselves, and indeed the Master now asked everyone to be careful and harmless. Careful even of the big emerald beetles that now had come out of hiding to watch and listen to the Master, these self-same beetles that people in our town usually just stomped on and squashed, and sometimes fried in hot oil to eat as a delicacy.

In this way, then, and for the first time in their lives, did the people of our small town find themselves sitting peacefully, and equally so, among creatures, and animals, and other wondrous little examples of life beings. And soon, newly arriving butterflies began alighting on their own heads, too.

3

TRYING TO FIND OUT ABOUT THE MASTER

Now, our small town is a good enough place, as so many are. But like other small towns everywhere, our people live within what's near and dear to them, and it's this that they understand best. Thus they might live their whole lives within what's near and dear to them, and indeed there's no apparent or urgent reason for them to do otherwise.

This, of course, is fine—until a Master with rainbow eyes comes along and sits in the park and talks to animals and other creatures as if they were equal to our town's citizens. And since everyone gathering could see this with their own eyes, they naturally marveled and wanted to know more about the Master.

But is this not natural? For newcomers always have to say what they are and where they've come from because this is what they're supposed to do in order to see how they fit in, and to reduce local worry about them. And so it became necessary to find out more about the Master, and this finding out went this way.

Many more were now arriving at the park to find out what was going on, and the sheriff now had something to do because it was up to him to keep order and to tell people where they should or should not sit or stand. And he also had to tell the newcomers not to stomp on the beetles because "he said not to."

And the three principal ladies found things they could do, too, since they now had talked to the Master longer than the newly arriving, and so it was up to these three to tell others what was going on.

"I think he's a saint of some kind," said the first principal lady, and she said this about to those who would listen.

But the second principal lady felt that "he's an angel in disguise." And so this was heard, too, by the newly gathering.

"Nonsense," exclaimed the third principal lady who was not particularly religious, "if anything, he may be a foreign master of some kind, and it's up to us to test him for his wisdom so that we can be sure he doesn't wreck our thought-substance and that of our children."

"So we must ask him who he is," said the first lady, and to this many heads nodded up and down.

So, the Master was asked: "Who are you, and what's your name?"

And he smiled again and said: "I don't need a name. I'm a merchant of harmlessness, as I've already said, and the names of the harmless are never remembered, so it's pointless for them to have names."

Well, the citizens of our town are not stupid. But even so they had never before heard of what the Master was now saying—and indeed someone from someplace else but with NoName surely seemed suspicious.

So this needed explaining, and so the Master continued:

"You see—if you can so see—the cruel, the mean, the destroyers, they have to have names so that they can be remembered in history because people have always paid them more attention than is given to the harmless. Violence, atrocity, conflict, even war, these are remembered the best because they bring about ruckuses, and so have to be focused on the most. The harmless don't make ruckuses, and so they need not be remembered. There is no history of the harmless, and so the names of the harmless are not needed. So the harmless pass through their lives without making much in the way of a ruckus, and so there's little to remember, and they are then forgotten, if even they did have names at one time."

At this, some one or two or a few more ladies began crying, and a wave of emotion spread through the now even larger crowd of those who had come to find out what was going on. "But," someone protested, "your view is so demoralizing. Surely there are enough genuinely good and harmless people among us?"

"Perhaps, perhaps," the Master nodded sagely. "But can you put a name to just one?"

As this small tendril of discussion worked its way through the crowd, combined with the attempts to put a name to someone who was not violent, and who truly was or had been harmless, someone finally agreed, seeming to speak for everyone, "it's difficult to put such a name to anyone."

So it was in this way that the people of our small town found themselves thinking of things they had never thought of before, and it seemed so natural to do so even though just moments ago most would have been troubled or embarrassed by such thinking.

The Master took a slight sip of the unpolluted water the

principal ladies had provided.

After a moment of silence the Master spoke again, "There has never been a gathering-together of harmlessness," the Master paused and then continued, "and so those among us that are full of harmlessness have no place to gather and indeed see no reason to gather themselves together."

"But," someone protested, "how can you be harmless in a world so full of harmfulness? After all, you need to fight back."

But the Master was serene and smiled again, and then said: "Trying to do as little harm as possible is a good start. All things, even harmlessness, have their beginnings—and when there are no beginnings then nothing is begun and so it cannot grow."

Now a large silence settled over the still growing crowd, and even newcomers sensed they should calm their hearts and their questions—especially when it was seen that some brilliant and glittering hummingbirds had arrived and were making a glorious circle just above the Master's head.

But then the third principal lady asked: "But if you have NoName, certainly you should tell us where you're from."

"I don't remember exactly," responded the Master, "it's been so long ago. It isn't very important anyway, though, because where you're going is always more important. Yet you can't know where you're going until you can see where it is."

But the same third principal lady wasn't to be dissuaded so easily. "Well, you're not very old, as your face shows, and surely you should remember something of your origins."

Again the Master smiled. "I can only remember what I do, and no one can remember what they can't. I'm older than I seem, far older indeed, and that I remember very well. But think upon this: in life and the air of love that supports it, what has age or the lack of it, to do with anything? The best thing to remember is life itself, not how old or young that life is—for all you have at any given time, is life."

So, at this point, who the Master was, and from where he had come, was not resolved. But the first principal lady, not wanting to be outdone by the third lady, now bluntly asked: "Well, then, are you immortal, or something?"

At this, the Master did not smile. But instead his rainbow eyes looked deeper into her own eyes for a while, and then cast a long look over the gathering crowd, and finally said: "This type of question is to be answered, if it is to be answered, only by yourself—for no one can either way say as much for anyone else."

But this questioning lady was not to be brushed aside so easily. "I don't understand this. Please explain yourself more fully."

"Madam, if you think about only what others think is thus and so, then shall you ever think for yourself, about yourself? Perhaps I can tell you much of what I've experienced on my long walking way. But this would only be passing conversation between us, and which merely whittles the time away."

Now this first principal lady was about to protest, but the Master went on. "At best, I am, like all and each of you here gathering, a wondrous life-unit and can have many names and identities depending on how and why I need them. But I need these not, for I'm searching for life, and the love that supports it, and what good are names, and identities, and from-wheres in all this. Life is. Love is. And with or without names they are."

Now, certainly, this was this no-answer, from this no-name Master, who couldn't remember how old he was. Our townspeople were not so stupid that they didn't realize the

Master was evading them not saying who he was, and from where.

But by now many in the crowd were themselves smiling at this evading because it's well known that each person wants others to know who they are, even if they themselves know not what they really are. Those more quick to understand began whispering:

"He's evading having an identity—which is what we all think we must have in order to feel ourselves to be real."

It's true that some in the growing gathering didn't exactly understand this motive. But since they could see that others did seem to understand it, or were smiling as if they did, those that didn't exactly comprehend remained silent in order not to be seen as too stupid.

As it ultimately turned out, although some remembered him as the Master of Harmlessness, who and wherefrom was this Master, was never discovered, and long after he had arrived, and departed, no one was any the wiser about this.

But this small question of who and wherefrom was shortly forgotten, and no longer worried about—for a new and more wonderful thing happened.

4

THE BEGINNING OF THE ILLUMINATION

With the question of who and wherefrom being left unresolved, someone in the growing gathering yelled out: "Why have you come to our town? Answer that, at least."

"Yes," immediately prompted the second principal lady, not wanting to be shoved aside by the first and third. "Our town is out of the way," she said, "it's small, and we are content and happy, and we manage our affairs very well."

The Master smiled, as usual. "I've come to your town because it's along the way from where I've come to where I'm going. Why else should anyone ever go anywhere unless it's for that? To get to where you want to go from where you were."

"But," protested this second principal lady, "this is no answer, either. Do you always speak in riddles?"

"No," grinned the Master, somewhat sheepishly some later said. "I never speak in riddles. Instead, I speak in illumination."

Now, in retrospect, it's relatively sure that no one in the growing gathering at first understood what this Master meant by these strange words. And this he knew, and so he went on. "You see, illumination is a kind of language, perhaps a forgotten one, but a language nonetheless, a kind of seeing-language."

At this, some few in the growing gathering grew restive, and felt they were tired of such talk, and who might blame them. But the Master went on anyway: "How can you see what's not lit up so that you *can* see it? Can you see things embedded in the dark, or enveloped in darkness? If you can't so see, then can you talk of what you don't see? Of course there are many ways of seeing, and thus of talking about what's seen. But there are many kinds of darkness, too, within which what's not seen can't be talked about—or not very well talked about at any rate."

Now did the second principal lady fidget, for it was she who has started all this up. So she said: "Well, for heaven's sake, give us an example of what you mean."

"Oh, yes," said the Master. "That's easy enough. You here gathering don't see how wondrous each and all of you are. And so you're not illuminated in this regard, and can't talk of yourselves as wondrous."

Now, it's generally true that people like to think themselves wonderful, and so whatever currents of flagging interest had gotten going now dissipated, and general interest was restored.

"But," persisted the second principal lady, "what does this have to do with your coming to our town? Have you come here to illuminate us?"

"Well, no, not exactly," smiled the Master—ever smiling it seemed. "I'm just passing through as I've said. People *do* pass through on their way to somewhere else. It's a simple, straightforward matter. But you were good enough to get me some pure water to drink, and I could repay this with a little illumination-language if you want. But I don't want to turn your town topsy-turvy. Illumination has a way of doing that."

Now someone shouted: "Ridiculous! Show us some illumination, then!" And a chanting then came from several, which said the same, and demanding a showing of illumination.

Then did the Master rise to his feet and open his arms a little. And at this, some later said, they felt a wave of tingling something, or other, but no one could ever be specific.

So, with his arms opening as if to embrace, the Master said: "Talk now among you of the flowers in this little park, and these you can see very well. You know these flowers need their seeds to begin them growing, and then need good earth, and good water, and the light of the daily sun overhead.

"And is this not what you think flowers are—seed, earth, water, sunlight? But how can seed, earth, water, and light do anything by themselves to make flowers? Yet this is the reality of flowers that you think, and believe, and teach that flowers are."

He paused and then recommenced, "And because you so believe, then this is all you can see of what flowers are. Is there not something more to flowers? Something you don't think, or believe, or teach, and which then you can't see because it's not real to you? Think Now! Think upon what's in the flower-seed, of its blueprint urge, and its pattern, and its energies for growing, which must be already in the seed, and which can't be seen by the eyes *until* it has grown and bloomed."

With this the Master paused and gathered onto himself

before he began again, "So talk now among you of the wonderful energies needed to sprout their seeds and then to grow, for nothing grows unless it's illuminated by its own indwelling and patterned energies. And when you talk of such, then will the flowers in this little park become illuminated, and then will you gathering here, see this illumination."

At this there was at first a shocked silence, but the Master went on: "Think, now, for you, all of you, can see in an illuminated way what you know to exist, and it's only what you don't think exists that remains dark to you and hidden from your sight."

At this point, some in the growing gathering began talking of the energy in seeds, the patterned energy which makes flowers grow and bloom in their final shape and beauty. And many then said that surely such energy-patterns must first exist in the seeds. For was not that what a seed was—a blueprinted energy pattern of some kind? And which, if such didn't exist, well then you could put the seed in the richest earth and pour water on it until the very last of days—and nothing would ever happen.

Was this not common sense?

Some said that surely it was, and that it was stupid to think otherwise. And as people talked this way among themselves, and then agreeing some with each other, and more with each another, then did some begin to see the energy of the flowers, and more then saw the same also.

And the flowers began illuminating their own inner energy-lights, and wonderful and delicate hues and tints sprouted into the air and scintillated like heat does, and the flowers themselves began glowing.

Some few did not see, of course, because they had been so strongly taught otherwise, and had been taught not to see what does exist. But their skeptical suspicions were soon submerged into the shoutings that now arose among the growing gathering, among those excited to now see something they had never seen before, and many had tears in their eyes—for all forms of beauty thus first seen bring tears.

"But how did you do this?" exclaimed the first principal lady through her marveling tears, and this she asked of the Master.

"I did nothing," responded the Master. "Are not those flower energies already there? It's you here gathering that understood something, something you would before not thought to make questions for. And in thus making this unasked question about how flowers can grow from their seeds, did not the answer present itself to your thought-substance seeing eyes?"

But many said that a miracle had occurred, the Miracle of the Flowers—to which the Master simply said: "Yes, flowers are a small thing of life, and all life is itself a miracle."

In any event, our small park was now a-glowing with the lights of the flowers, and when people considered the seeds of trees, then too did the nearby trees begin illuminating in one beautiful way or another, and many glorious lights and auroras bathed the entire surroundings.

And these glorious lights and auroras were of the colors blue and glowing green, burning red, and dark brown, and of other hues and tints, too, just like the Master's own rainbow eyes.

5

THE MASTER SPEAKS ABOUT "THE WAY"

And now also had the news that a Master was in our park spread from our small town into the surrounding countryside, and to places beyond that. And so people left their work near and far, and rushed into our small town to see what was to be seen of all this. And soon our few streets were clogged with arriving people.

But the sheriff knew what to do to keep order and crowd control, and went here and there shouting this and that. Some enterprising person, or two, brought up a loud-speaker and set it going whence it whined and grumbled at first.

Now, the third principal lady could be heard far and near, and the other two ladies as well, and of course the words of the Master could be heard likewise. "But how can we ask questions we've not thought of to get answers we know nothing about?"

To this the Master responded. "The hardest part of life doesn't revolve around finding answers which exist in plenty, but in asking the right questions. Answers to questions not asked remain unknown, and so nothing of their answers can be seen or illuminated."

"Well, if you *are* a Master," complained the third principal lady, "then you're a very puzzling one. How can we ask questions that we don't know exist to be asked?"

"Oh," smiled the Master. "That's easy enough. Just wonder about what you don't know about, but which would be important to you, not to anyone else. Perhaps then neither questions nor answers will be as important as they seem."

But the first principal lady was not so easily to be put off. So she demanded: "Master—and here now was this venerable title used for the first time—if you are one, and this you must be because you can command the animals, then aren't masters supposed to show us the way?"

Now returned the smile to the Master's face. "Kind soul, the only way anyone will ever find is that which each finds of and in themselves. The ways found by others for themselves might be discussed, perhaps for comparing them. But will you embark upon another's way? A way not discovered within yourself, but discovered by another, or taught by another? The *Ways of Life and Love* are not like the ways on a map going from city to city, or between town and town."

The first principal lady wanted to interrupt, but the Master went on.

"Are *you* not *already* a way of and in yourself?"

Now there was an obvious and monumental silence, largely because no one knew what to say, since they now knew, only if vaguely.

"What good are the ways of others, even those of masters, if you *first* don't realize what your already-indwelling life-way is all about? How can you try to look at the many ways of life outside of you, without first looking at yourself, and your Way?"

Now the Master smiled as if in some kind of joy: "One of the funny things about all our lives is that when we look chiefly at what's outside of us, then we actually begin to see *less* of what's out there. And this is easy enough to prove. For if you find something indwelling in you, which you'd not seen before, then how you see what's outside of you will be seen differently, and even more so."

At this, the Master suddenly closed his rainbow eyes, as if tired from his speaking—and who by now could blame him for this tiredness. But by now many in the crowd gathering had begun sensing their own motions, and some had said "Yes, I can see my Way better now and more clearly so." And then did many more say as much of themselves.

6

THE MASTER'S "LIFE-UNIT" MESSAGE

Some people now were heard grumbling, and some wanted to leave the growing gathering, and made pretense of so doing. But those found they didn't really want to leave even though the Master's words and concepts were complicated and confusing.

Now the first principal lady said to the Master: "All you've said seems complicated. We here in this small town are only average but sturdy people, and we take pride in that. How can we find our own Ways, and see them pure and simple? Answer us that one thing. Show us an example of what you mean."

The Master sighed, and opened his eyes, now glowing golden as two suns—and for the first time everyone, or most of them, saw his eyes in the same way. "Consider this: Is there not an average and sturdy idea of what people are? And is not this idea first and foremost those physical bodies that come into birth?"

And so this was discussed a little among the growing gathering, and most said "Yes," this is what people are. A few, though, said they were spirit first and foremost, and then body only second.

"Now," the Master went on, "body and spirit are things both true enough. But neither of these two true things refer to something even more important to them. And it is this: body and spirit are both forms, or aspects of, the greater essence of life itself. Body and spirit are thus drawn from the greater essence of life. And if not body or spirit contain this life-essence, then would they exist as life? And without this life-essence, would babes be born and then grow into what you are, and listening to me and yourselves?"

And the Master continued: "Consider this! Seed and egg don't make life, but themselves are expressions of life, itself, continuing through them, and their mixing."

The Master paused, "No. Is it not that life comes *before* spirit and body can be, it is *out of* that life that spirit and body are built, and this is as sure as is anything, and everything, built out of something else."

Now the crowd gathering, still growing, was silent and thoughtful, and this quietness persisted until someone (it was never found out who) asked in a meek voice: "Then are we life *before* we are spirit or our bodies?"

To this the Master smiled, and said: "How can life be where the essence of life does not first exist? Wherever the essence of life does not first exist, then nothing of life is produced. Are not your bodies and spirit products *of* life? Being things life itself has produced?"

Now there was a profound silence that came to over-cover the crowd-gathering with thoughtfulness, and many wondered in this, or that different direction, for some while. But after this silence and wondering had gone on perhaps too long, the Master began drumming his fingers on his bench and finally said: "Is it not that life is the horse that pulls and draws the carts of your spirit and bodies? This arrangement is not the other way around. For how could it be the other way around, even if this other-way-around is the average and sturdy idea of what you are?"

Now some few of the here-gathered began weeping, but others began laughing and chuckling, and now the Master pounced: "First there is life, then there are units in this life, and then these life-units become spirit and thence become bodies. So are you not life-units before spirit and body?"

Many nodded their heads up and down, but many others were yet unsure and uncertain. "Well, then," the Master continued, "if you think of yourselves as body, then won't your realities depend upon, and be decided by, this thinking? But if realities are based on being first a life-unit, a unit of life and its essence, then will not the realities be decided differently? And even be *seen* differently?"

But still many were yet unsure and uncertain, and some grumbled as might be expected. And some newcomers lately arriving at the group gathering asked "What is he talking about?" And yet other newcomers asked: "Why should he speak only of what we can already understand?"

"After all," they said, "if the Master tells us about what we already know, then what real use is he, and why should he come at all?"

The three principal ladies agreed with this, and the second lady said that everything seems complicated if we don't know about it. And "Yes," said the third lady, "it's only after you find out about it that it seems easier and more simple."

So a committee to question the Master formed up, and questions were to be compared and selected mostly by majority rule, and only after suitable questions had been found, only these then would be asked of the Master.

And so it was found out there were no good questions, since most people could ask about only what they already knew about. And why ask a Master about these? Surely a Master, if he is one, should speak about things not already known.

Furthermore, some in the committee said that the only things that can be taught are what someone already knows about. This led to the same situation of only dealing within the already-known-about. And so someone then said that perhaps the Master should be asked about things that no one knows anything about.

And the three principal ladies nodded in agreement, and a silence came over the crowd gathering while one and all awaited the Master to again open his resting rainbow eyes.

This he shortly did, and his opening eyes were now something like the glowing flowers in which the bees were nestled. And so the first principal lady said: "Tell us what you will, but only what none of us here gathered know nothing about."

"Yes," said the Master. "I will then tell you of three things, and after this I must be again on my way to another place ahead. Let me then tell of how beautiful and wonderful each and all of you are, from the most intelligent to the most stupid, for all of you are magnificent and astonishing."

7

THE MASTER SPEAKS ABOUT THE MIRACULOUS

Now the Master stood to his feet from his resting, and in doing so it seemed he grew in size and height—not so very much, of course, but he became somehow larger than all who had gathered—and yet he remained the same, too.

"Think, now," he began, "of how beautiful and wonderful you are—for if it is not this that you think upon, then what's worthwhile left to think upon at all?"

At this, many who might not have been thinking themselves beautiful and wonderful, as many don't, nonetheless began trying to see themselves as such—or at least think upon it in some small way.

The Master then continued: "Think now of the wonders of your biological bodies, those very exquisite things that are taken for granted and viewed as expendable by many who would use them for purposes other than those of harmlessness."

The Master let this sink in and then resumed, "The human bio-body, as are all bio-bodies, as are those of plants and creatures and flying wonders, all are miracles of structure and function. Are these not put together in ways that are inexplicable. And are they not delicate, yet strong, and do they not do what they do without us having to tell them thus and so about what to do?

"First there is the skin that you see, but beneath that are muscles and bone, all laced together with nerves and chemical and electrical codes, and then beneath these are bones built from the calcium of earth itself.

"And are there then not the internal organs, which sometimes disgust the dainty-minded? Think upon these, and see that nonetheless all of them do more than one function and maintain the bio-life processes that you, all of you, value so much.

"And are not all these bio-things made up of trillions of active and ever-changing cells and atoms all working together and knowing by themselves what to do, and do so even though you don't know at all that they are doing so?

"Here then is a wonder beyond compare—and if this wonder beyond compare is not held together by beauty of form and function, then ask what otherwise will hold it together.

"You know that if you touch and admire your skin, your face, and caress them with your hands and your eyes in mirrors, then you know they become more beautiful.

"But in your seeing thus, you can likewise touch and admire all of your bio-body's forms and functions, and none of these can be ugly because all of them work to maintain the physical life you so much value and desire. And is not this life beautiful, and if it is so beautiful, then can anything that sustains it be ugly?

"Hold up now your hands before your face and eyes. And ask these hands to show their skeleton bones, and their running nerves, and these will appear to you in your seeing. And as the flowers glowing hereby are illuminating up, then too does not your hand seen this way illuminate up?"

Thus did everyone in the crowd-gathered hold up their arms and hands to try to see as much, and this vast communal gesture of uprising interest created something strange: a tremulous sound like communal breath, and a soft rumbling thunder as if the sky above might crack open.

But the Master continued: "See, now, that if all of you altogether decide to see the bio-body's beauty, its wonders of form and function—then cannot more of you see into your bodies, and are not those bio-bodies remarkable and extraordinary things in their wondrous form and functions?

"But indeed, how many of you live within this perfected and perfect bio-body thing and know not that it's your nearest miracle of life and living? Yes, all of you are living within a miracle, and if you can't perceive this first miracle, then how will you perceive all those other miracles around you? Indeed, it takes a miracle to see other miracles, for only the miraculous can see and find one another. And is not seeing itself a miracle?

"And miracles seeing each other bring into existence that which sustains them altogether—but what that is I'll not tell you, for if you can't find it yourselves along your life-units' ways, then what real good does it do merely to say what it is?"

At this, the Master again closed his energy-eyes and rested in repose. But by now some few, and then some few more, had begun looking with new seeing at those standing next to and around them, and some at least realized that they were standing next to a bio-body miracle—and which before they had seen as just another person, and not as a miracle at all.

Then slowly but surely did begin to form an opening-up-emotion of the miraculous—and shortly, as if an orifice of love slowly turning and expanding and expanding and turning with many gentle illuminations, then this opening-up enveloped the entire crowd-gathering, and many thought and spoke out that miracles must have love in order to perceive each other, for without this love are not sight and seeing blind?

And then some said that if one cannot see what's to be loved, then there's only to be seen what isn't to be loved—and those not-to-be-loved things then become the only things seen around them—and those not-to-be-loved things are not miracles—and then where else is there to live and abide but in a miracle-less place—and in that miracle-less place none can see themselves as miraculous even though they are body, spirit, and life-essence itself.

And none of this did the Master need to tell them, for the people group-gathered-together figured it out for themselves. And this was as it should be, for what each one can't figure out for self cannot really exist for that one in any other real way.

8

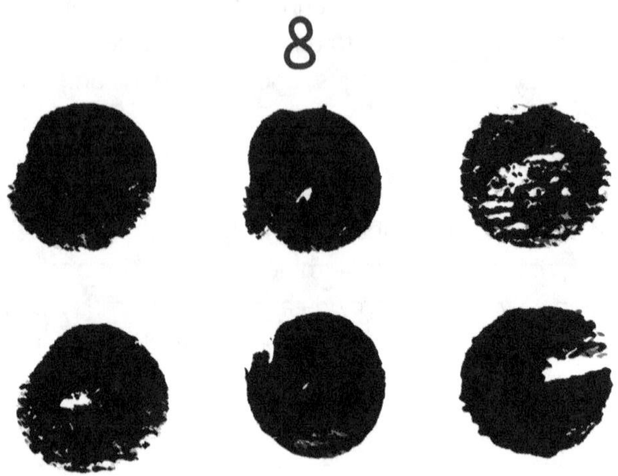

THE EXTRUDING OF THE DEMONS
AND THE CLEANSING

Now came about in our little park yet another exceedingly strange thing, and it was this. Some demons were seen to appear here and there among the gathering, and as these first few appeared then did more and more appear until there was a plenty of them. These demons were of all colors and shapes and sizes, but generally small enough to have fitted into peoples' hearts or minds or wherever else fitted such demons as these.

Hate, intolerance, suspicion, and anger were seen because it was easy enough to identify them. But others, unknown demons, appeared also, very strange creations indeed, and no one really knew what they were or signified. And all of these demons appeared encased in sticky dark-light bubbles of some kind, and those bubbles floated here and there, but could find no place to stick and lodge themselves.

Some of the many people gathered were at first afraid of those demons encased in their dark bubbles and looking sheepish and embarrassed. And the sheriff didn't know exactly what to do, since he now had to deal with these demons as well as the small creatures and beetles, and then the gathered people, too.

First there were expressions of fear and disgust because of these demons, but soon some people giggled or laughed at them—and some daring few kicked some of those bubbles back and forth as if in a game of kicking back and forth. Again the sheriff was perplexed since he didn't know if it was legal or illegal to kick demons about in this playful way.

At this the Master once more opened his rainbow eyes, and now those eyes were ruby red and glowing mightily, as if burning like narrow beams and strings of light through one and all. And then the Master spoke once more.

"And now you here gathered ask where these demons have come from, and why they're here in the first place."

No one had really asked this, of course, but it seemed like a good question and no one of the committee protested it. So the Master went on: "I'll ask *you* if the demon of hate is a miracle? And I'll ask if the demon of intolerance is a miracle? And I'll ask this so forth of all these demons, whether you recognize them or not."

Then was there some consternation among the group-gathered, for now the Master was asking questions of those questioning him. And no one knew at first how or what to answer back to him.

But then the first principle lady cried out and pointed at a certain dark-light bubble floating here and there: "Well, I recognize *that* particular demon of hate, because it is mine, and I see that demon is formed out of all the hatred I've experienced and encountered."

And as the first principal lady pointed to that particular bubble, and said as much of it—well, that bubble popped, and the demon inside of it vanished.

At this, some few others began pointing to their own demons floating encased in certain dark-light bubbles, and then more and more did the same—and finally there were lots of popping dark-light bubbles, and more and more of these plentiful demons vanished into thin air.

But the first principal lady was frowning throughout all this popping and vanishing of demons, and she continued to frown until she finally said: "But from where else did form this, my own demon of hatred, unless it formed within me?"

Pausing to reflect, she thought out loud, "Have I then made it up and stuck it together in my own thought-substance?"

At this the Master laughed. "Ask not from where or by how such demons are formed, for then you'll become sunk and lost in the intricacies of demonology. But ask whether your own demon of hatred, or any other demon of whatever kind, has a place in the realm of the miraculous of which your own wondrous self is part and parcel before you can in your mind form this or that demon."

But before anyone could answer, the Master went on: "Ask if demons are miraculous. Ask if they make miracles. Ask if they are part of the miraculous—ask if they are a part of life—ask if they are part of the love-energies that sustain life."

Now was there an extending silence over the group-gathered, a sort of soft silence except for demon-bubbles continuing to pop here and there. Now was this silence as no one knew what to say, and many were still very astonished to see their demons floating.

So the Master continued: "Ask these questions of

yourself, and in so asking you'll soon see that demons can't find an easy existence within the miraculous realms, those selfsame realms of which each and all of you are first and foremost a life-unit part."

At this, there arose from the gathering, a noise of giggling embarrassment—for many more were now realizing from where these demons had come and arisen.

But now appeared more ferocious and bigger mega-demons, also encased in sticky dark-light bubbles. And these new demons were ominous, and dark, and had thunder and lightning about them. But in general, they were a pitiful lot, and sadness could be seen dripping from their tired eyes. And the bigger demon-bubbles of this sadness-dripping lot had multitudes of long snake-like sticky whips extending out from them, and it was obvious that those sticky whips were trying to stick into the thought-substances of those in the group-gathered.

At the appearance of these mega-demons most in the gathered were now quite afraid, and some cowered. But a few of the brave again laughed and pointed out the demons of war and abomination and holocaust and Armageddon—and all of these, and more of them that no one recognized, indeed were awful and dismal and pathetic.

Now the second principal lady wailed: "But from where are these mega-demons from? I don't think they are made up in my own thought-substance, for I've never seen such as these at all. They must have been put together by someone else."

To this the Master replied: "Are not war and holocaust and other atrocious mega-demons always put together or made up artificially, for these are not miraculous as you know? The not-miraculous always has to be invented, and so what's not miraculous always is a put-together thing—and this whether it be in the thought-substance of individuals, or in groups of them, and then the many."

At this the second principal lady said: "Are you saying that we communally create such mega-demons, and do so without knowing that we do?"

But before the second principal lady could go on the Master said: "I say nothing, for such of my sayings then would merely be a teaching that some might believe in but in which others would not believe."

But the second principal lady went on thoughtfully. "It may be," she said, "that those who like war and such, well it may be that it's they who invent such demons—and these demons grow excessively big and powerful among those who like war and such, and finally such mega-demons find ways to stick their tendrils into all and everyone."

But the Master then went on: "Consider not wherefrom arise such mega-demons, for such wherefrom is very complex and intricate. But consider whether such mega-demons are miraculous or not."

Now, the third principal lady, once more not wanting to be left out, said: "Well, war and other such whatnot is not miraculous, not astounding, and so such mega-demons can only be sustained and vivified by those dwelling in some non-miraculous state of thinking."

It was at this epiphany from the third principal lady that many began nodding their heads up and down—and with this the big bubbles surrounding the horrible mega-demons themselves began popping. Rather they sort of *exploded*, since they were too big merely to pop. And when they so exploded then were terrible stinks and other foul odors smelled, which revolted most in the gathering.

But now the gathered multitudes of butterflies and bees and other flying little creatures fanned their wings altogether and at the same time, and a small breeze was thus made, and this breeze blew away the stinks and the foul odors.

When such stinks had been blown away by the many tiny wings, the Master resumed: "You see, then, that even mega-demons must extrude and vanish when there is a big group effort to dwell in the miraculous, as the wondrous things each and all of you are. For such mega-demons cannot find a place to stick onto in the realms of the miraculous. For they are *not* a natural part of such miraculous realms—not miraculous as are each and all of you here gathered, and all of whom are first and foremost miraculous to begin with."

Then said the sheriff, who was relieved that the demons had popped and exploded on their own: "Miraculous-ness and Non-miraculous-ness are not made of the same stuff. Is that what you're saying? Miraculous-ness and Non-miraculous-ness don't fit together, do they, unless you together combine and sustain them yourself?"

But the Master merely smiled for a while, and then said in a small voice which would have escaped the gathered crowd save for the loudspeakers: "And neither do harmlessness and harmfulness fit together and in the same way you've just said."

But before this could be dealt with and understood very well, someone shouted: "Is this not a cleansing!"

And most agreed that it was a cleansing, for with so many poppings and explodings all was now cleaner. And so it must have been a cleansing everyone now agreed, for now the very air around was sparkling and glittering, and people gathered began breathing in the sparkles—although every once in a while a new demon extruded into view, only to be playfully kicked around until it popped and vanished.

In the end it was more or less communally decided that no great interest need to be paid to demons, and when this was generally agreed to then did the demons stop appearing.

For demons neither are formed nor appear unless there is interest in them, for it is this interest-essence they feed upon and grow from, and not the essences of love and life and marvelous miraculous-ness and harmlessness.

And people began saying that this was so simple, and they then wondered why they had not, in this simple way, understood it before.

9

THE APPEARANCE OF THE ANGELS

But now, and without hardly any time to adjust to the absence of demons, a new thing came about. And it came about this way.

Now that all those demons, of varying colors and shapes and forms, had popped or exploded, the committee once again wanted to decide upon which questions should be posed to the Master. But although there was much talking, well, that committee found that there were not as many questions to ask as there had been before the demons extruded.

Instead, many in the crowd gathered were not very interested in asking questions because it was more interesting to look and see what people looked like after the demons had been extruded. And thus many were heard saying to one another: "Well, I hardly recognize you without your demons."

But many were now very playful, and said back: "Well. It may instead be that you hardly recognize me without *your* demons."

But in the end it didn't matter which way this was, for soon it was very widely agreed that things, and what everyone looked, were more wonderful without demons, and there was now no need to think or ask about where or why they had come.

But it was just then that some of those gathered began noticing, in the crowd, the faces of some exceptionally beautiful people. Those exceptionally beautiful faces were floating among those gathered, and some, or even most of them, were just shining faces, and nothing else.

At first some were a little afraid of such floating faces with nothing else attached beneath them, not even necks, even though those floating faces did smile radiantly at everyone. But shortly some of those floating faces developed bodies beneath them, and some of these were dressed in glorious clothes that sparkled as if made up only of sparkling lights.

And then some, but not all of them, sprouted wings of blue and golden rays and lights, and it was if these wings had been made out of the air around. And these wings waved slowly enveloping this or that person in blue and golden light, and as they were so enveloped those persons' feet left the ground and they floated somewhat into the air above.

But not all of these beautiful faces developed wings, for some were wingless. But from their gorgeous eyes of those wingless shown soft piercing shafts of multi-colored rays, and those rays went into and through people here and there, and even the smiles of these wingless shown forth with soft waves of light that cascaded and touched very many in the gathering.

And then it was seen that those faces and wings and rays and smiles did pass transparently through the faces and bodies of the people gathered. And wherever there was such a passing through, the air around lit up with sparkles, and shortly the entire gathering was lit up with such sparkles because of so many passing throughs.

But the first principal lady was perplexed, even though she had been shown through and lighted up and felt as if verging on levitating ecstasy. She asked of the Master: "What now are these? Are these not *angels* of some kind?"

But the Master was disinterested. "Ask *me* nothing, but rather look and study what you are seeing—and do so until you find out something and understand."

And so the first principal lady looked harder and more intently, and almost everyone else did likewise. And after some looking here and there at the beautiful faces, well, the first principal lady cried out: "Look at that one!" and she pointed at one of the angelic faces near her. And so everyone looked, and when they did it could be seen that the face resembled the principal first lady, but in a more refined and beautiful way.

"Why," cried out the first lady, "why, that is me, that beautiful face—only, well, it's a better me—but it is me nonetheless."

And so the first lady turned to the Master and said: "I suppose that this is a part of me, an aspect of me. But it is no longer imprisoned within me." And the Master was about to answer her but there was now a swelling commotion of joy as many others found themselves reflected in the faces of this or that angelic vision floating here and there.

So immense was this joy that the Master, so that he could be heard, pressed the microphone closer to his soft lips and flowing beard and said: "Well, with so many demons popped and exploded why should your angelic selves stay imprisoned and unseen within. What in the first place has caused these angelic selves to stay imprisoned and unseen?"

And so once more the Master was questioning those who would question him—and was this not as it should be? For do not the answers lie within the questioner to begin with?

So the second principal lady laughed with joy and said back to the Master: "You are a tricky Master, aren't you? Look at my manifold self, and how beautiful are all my angelic parts now that we can see them!"

"Yes, indeed," responded the Master. "But now ask yourself this: would not a life-unit be beautiful, since all life is beautiful in some way? Can you conceive of a life-unit being ugly and awful to begin with?"

Again everyone gathered began nodding up and down their manifold and beautiful faces, all of which were smiling and glittering aspects of themselves.

And so the third principal lady chimed in: "Yes, oh Yes! How could a life-unit ever begin by being ugly and awful, for it would then not live at all, would it?"

To which the Master replied: "Well, indeed that must be so, for all life must be harmonious within itself, and so all life-units must be harmonious to begin with—and this is so since life that begins as disharmony can't possibly get along very far."

"Yes, oh Yes!" now shouted the crowd gathered in our town's small park, and then many went on shouting a number of things, but the gist of which was this, and many spoke these exact same words: "How can what's disharmonious live very long? And if it does live for some little time, what can it manifest except disharmony and even destruction."

To this the Master smiled and reminded: "And such disharmonious, short-lived life will manifest harmfulness, too, for what is not harmonious is disharmonious and is therefore harmful to whatever is harmonious."

But by this time, and while many were thinking their way through all of this, the feet of all those gathered were now lifted off from our small park's ground or walks or lawns. And the Master himself was now floating above his bench.

And most of those gathered could now see that the Master had a thousand angelic faces and that each of these had eyes of different colors and hues and tints.

And now many realized why each person had seen eyes different in color, and this was because each person had in some way seen a different angelic aspect of the Master.

But it was at this point that yet another most wondrous thing happened. For the sky above opened up, and a brilliant, even brittle musical light struck out in all directions. But it was a soft and glorious light, golden and pink in nature, and from within this light descended what everyone instantly recognized to be angels proper—largely because their wings and winglets and rays and lights, both large and small, and in between, were indescribable.

With so many angels descending did their wings beat the air until the branches and leaves of the trees around our small park thought there was a storm going on and moved themselves accordingly.

But for the trees swaying and sighing, yet there was ultimate calm and tranquility in our small park.

And by now there was so much light here and there and coming from all directions of different colors and different rays and auroras that no one knew, or cared, anymore where it did or didn't come from.

And those angels did descend from above, and descended until they had come down and mixed with, and into, the crowd gathered.

And there were great flocks of these angels, big and

small, and no one gathered was afraid, for there was nothing left to be afraid of.

10

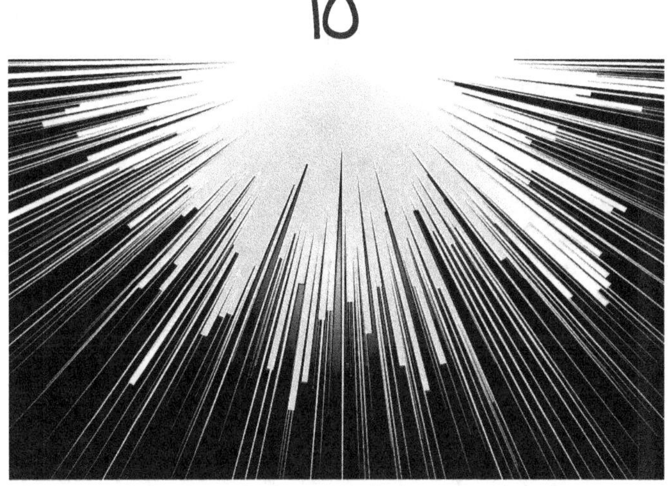

THE COMMUNION AND THE RAPTURE

And by now with so many angels coming down and descending into and among the angelic aspects of all those gathered, and the feet of all those gathered floating above our small park, did yet another thing happen.

What this thing was is hard to describe, and it may be that none but the completely harmless will ever know what it was. Many later described it in different ways. But however it was differently described didn't really matter very much— for each person describing it, however differently, did recognize the descriptions of all the others.

And so what now happened was a thing that can be described in many ways. But the general, and the particular, essence of what happened is this.

Light has a way of illuminating what it does, and whatever is illuminated had been in the darkness before, because if that's not where it was then there's no need to illuminate it. And so to understand what happened, the question must be asked, and it was thus asked by the Master: "Wherefore and whatever is it that now needs illumination?"

But even though the Master asked this, most in the crowd gathered were not paying much attention because, well, for one thing, those gathered communally understood that love does not ask questions, nor have need of words. No, its essence is felt, and someone or anyone feels it or doesn't feel it. Those that feel love need no words for it, while there are not enough words to explain it to those who don't feel it.

"Yes," smiled the Master of Harmlessness sensing the communal understanding, "only those who don't feel love ask for it to be described to them."

Of course, the pink light and rays and sparkles that both grew out of the crowd gathered and also descended was the pink light of love—for love is always described as soft and pink, or at least rosy enough.

"And that must be true, too," said the Master. And he went on: "Try, for example, imagining green love, or blue love, or yellow love, or orange love. No, these lights belong to other things."

Furthermore, all of us gathered began asking each other and ourselves, is not love always felt as some kind of ecstasy and rapture? And within ecstasy-feeling and rapture-feeling what need are there of questions or words?

"And yes," agreed the Master. "Yes, this is so, too, for are there not miraculous things that have no need of questions or words?"

And besides, we all said among ourselves, there are other ways of communicating and communing beside those of word-ways, and this is as everyone knows, even though they sometimes don't pay enough attention in this regard.

And so at some point when there's sufficient light to illuminate everything, sufficient harmlessness so that all that is of life itself doesn't get stepped on too much, and sufficient love to enfold all that happens—and when all of these are enough-shared by many, then what is it that *must* transpire among and between the many so sharing all of this?

"Yes, oh Yes," everyone sensed the Master saying, "think on this yourself, for I'll not answer it. For this answer is in yourself, as it always has been in all life-units since the first moment of their becoming units drawn from the greater luminosity of life itself and the love that sustains them."

In any event, in our town a big glow of light emanated suddenly upward and outward from our small park, and this glow spread momentarily far and wide, and was seen miles away.

But if you were in our small park when this big glow burst forth, then you would not have seen it save as you were part of it. For now all those gathered in that small park were, so to speak, momentarily disappeared within the communal light and rays and sparkles of life and love which is, and was, and always will be, their basic selves, no matter how many demons they otherwise make-up.

And to know this for sure of one's self and of and between all others is communion and rapture. And nothing of real life, or not much of it, is to be found in any other circumstance.

THE DEPARTURE OF THE MASTER

At some point in all of this communion and rapture, and bursting outward and upward of light and rays and sparkles, did the Master put down the microphone. But he did so in ways that didn't attract attention—except that the three principal ladies, always watching everything, did notice.

And when they raised their eyebrows, the Master did then say to them, but quietly so: "I'm rested enough now in your good and small park, and so I'll be on my way to where I'm going."

And the Master softly said this as well to the creatures and butterflies and beetles as well as to the people gathered and the angels descended, and said as much to the glowing flowers and undulating trees as well.

But the first principal lady rolled her eyes and said: "You call this rest?"

"Well, yes," responded the Master. "Is it not restful?"

At this, and not to be outdone, the second and third

principal ladies opened their mouths to say something additional. But the Master stood up taller than before, and as they watched, did his body grow indistinct, and continued growing more and more indistinct, until only his rainbow eyes were left.

And those eyes watched the three principal ladies for a moment, and then for a longer moment watched everyone else, too. And those multi-colored eyes were smiling, for eyes can smile as well as lips.

And then those rainbow eyes of the Master vanished, too.

Thus, and in this way, did the Master of Harmlessness come into our town, wherein he rested for a while in our small park. And while he so rested in our small park, he told us something about our real selves, and after that he went on along his *Way* from where he had come to somewhere else.

***

A BioMind Superpowers Book from
Swann-Ryder Productions, LLC

www.ingoswann.com

<u>OTHER BOOKS BY INGO SWANN</u>

Everybody's Guide to Natural ESP
Penetration
Penetration: Special Edition Updated
Preserving the Psychic Child
Psychic Literacy
Psychic Sexuality
Purple Fables
Reality Boxes
Resurrecting the Mysterious
Secrets of Power, Volume 1
Secrets of Power, Volume 2
Star Fire
The Great Apparitions of Mary
The Windy Song
The Wisdom Category
Your Nostradamus Factor

www.ingramcontent.com/pod-product-compliance
Lightning Source LLC
Chambersburg PA
CBHW071841190726
48292CB00005B/1856